She's My Mommy Too!

An Alaskan Tale of Sibling Rivalry

by Bernd and Susan Richter
Illustrated by Diane L. Drashner

Published by
Saddle Pal Creations, Inc., Wasilla, Alaska, USA

It was a cold Alaska Christmas night shimmering
with northern lights when our trusted sled dog Sasha
had her seven puppies. They were so, so cute, and
Sasha was a great mother to each and everyone.
But the puppies grew up to be the jealous kind.
Each one now wants Mommy all to itself.

First there is Lilly,
who is a bit silly.

She is lean and tall
and likes to play ball.

But when she wants to play with her mother,
there come cries from her sisters and brother:
"Me, Me, Me, Me, Me, Me - not YOU!",
to which Lilly replies:
"Don't be jealous, she's My Mommy TOO!"

Next there is Daisy,
who is a bit lazy.
Her only desire
is to sleep near the fire.

But when she wants to sleep next to mother,
there come cries from her sisters and brother:
"Me, Me, Me, Me, Me, Me - not YOU!",
to which Daisy replies:
"Don't be jealous, she's My Mommy TOO!"

**Then there is Fay,
with fur long and gray.**

**She is so quick and able,
she can jump onto the table.**

But when she jumps along with her mother,
there come cries from her sisters and brother:
"Me, Me, Me, Me, Me, Me - not YOU!",
to which Fay replies:
"Don't be jealous, she's My Mommy TOO!"

And now for Skeeter,
who is a big eater.
She loves everything sour and sweet,
from chocolate ice cream to pickled pigs feet.

But when she shares a meal with her mother,
there come cries from her sisters and brother:
"Me, Me, **Me**, Me, Me, Me - not YOU!",
to which Skeeter replies:
"Don't be jealous, she's My Mommy TOO!"

We can't forget Puff,
who likes to play rough.
She chases squirrels and cats,
and even frisbees and hats.

**But when she plays chase with her mother,
there come cries from her sisters and brother:
"Me, Me, Me, Me, Me, Me - not YOU!",
to which Puff replies:
"Don't be jealous, she's My Mommy TOO!"**

And here is our Gail,
with a big bushy tail.
She loves to roam
far away from home.

But when she roams afar with her mother,
there come cries from her sisters and brother:

**And last of all is big Max,
who is sturdy as an ax.**

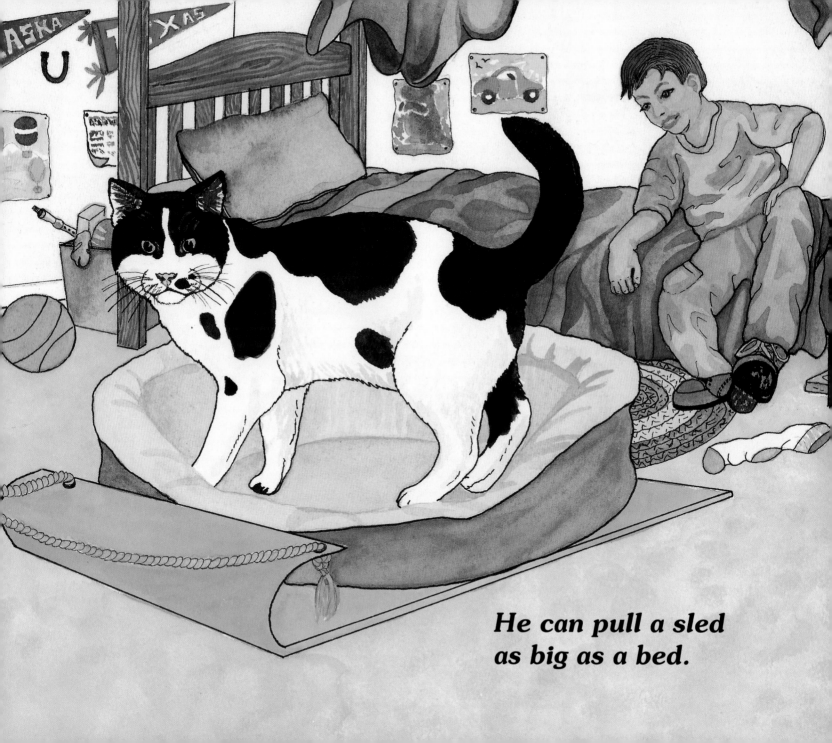

*He can pull a sled
as big as a bed.*

But when he pulls the sled with his mother,
his sisters cry to each other:
"Me, Me, Me, Me, Me, Me - not YOU!",
to which Max replies:
"Don't be jealous, she's My Mommy TOO!"

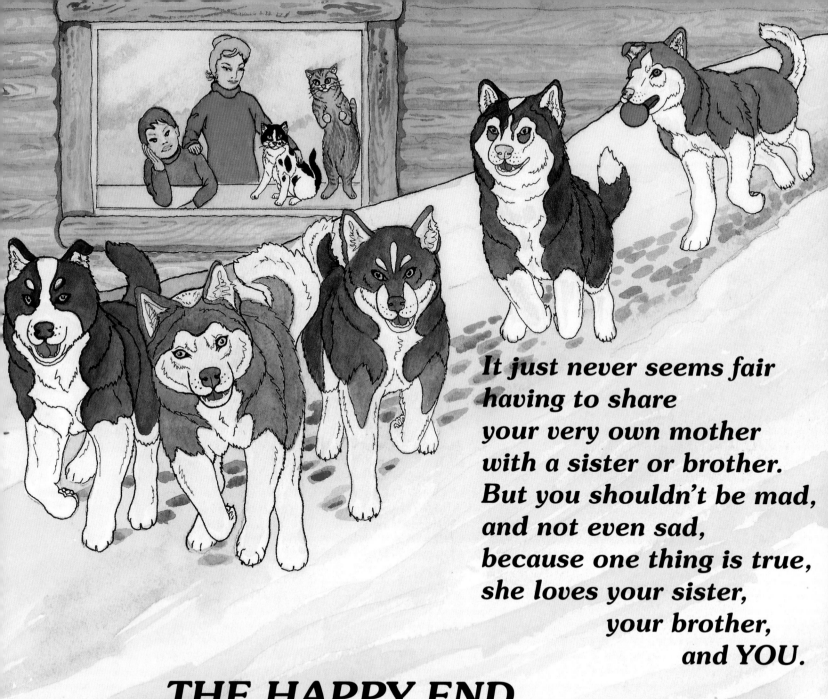

It just never seems fair
having to share
your very own mother
with a sister or brother.
But you shouldn't be mad,
and not even sad,
because one thing is true,
she loves your sister,
your brother,
and YOU.

THE HAPPY END

Acknowledgements:
We owe special thanks to Linda Thurston for her editing efforts and suggestions.
Thanks also to Danae Drashner, Jan O'Meara, Betty Hunter, and Wray Kinard.

"Dedicated to Max, Scooter, Kobuk, Smudgy, Lilly, Kiska & Xena." - B.&S.Richter
"Dedicated to my kids and grandkids - the joys of my life." - D.L.Drashner

Text and publication copyright © 2005 by Bernd and Susan Richter
Illustration copyright © 2005 by Diane L Drashner
Third Printing; Printed in China, July 2012
ISBN # 1-931353-15-8
Designed, produced, published and distributed in Alaska by:
  Bernd & Susan Richter
  Saddle Pal Creations, Inc.
  P.O. Box 872127
  Wasilla, Alaska, 99687-2127; USA

More children's books and games by Bernd and Susan Richter, Saddle Pal Creations, Inc.:

* A Bus Ride Into Denali (folding book)
* Alaska Animals - Where Do They Go At 40 Below?
* Alaskan Toys - For Girls and Boys
* Cruising Alaska's Inside Passage
* Discover Alaska's Denali Park
* Do Alaskans Live in Igloos?
* Good Morning Alaska - Good Morning Little Bear
* Goodnight Alaska - Goodnight Little Bear
* Grandma and Grandpa Cruise Alaska's Inside Passage
* Grandma and Grandpa Love Their RV
* Grandma and Grandpa Ride the Alaska Train
* Grandma and Grandpa Visit Denali National Park
* How Alaska Got its Flag (with Alaska flag song CD)
* How Animal Moms Love Their Babies
* I See You Through My Heart (Lift-the-Flap book)
* Listen to Alaska's Animals (sound book)
* Listen to the Alaska Train (sound book)
* My Alaska Animals - Can You Name Them?

* Peek-A-Boo Alaska (Lift-the-Flap book)
* She's My Mommy Too!
* The Little Bear Who Didn't want to Hibernate
* The Twelve Days of Christmas in Alaska
* There Was a Little Bear
* There Was a Little Porcupine
* Touch and Feel Alaska's Animals
* Traveling Alaska
* Uncover Alaska's Wonders (Lift-the-Flap book)
* When Grandma and Grandpa Cruised Through Alaska
* When Grandma and Grandpa Rode the White Pass Train
* When Grandma and Grandpa Rode the Alaska Train
* When Grandma and Grandpa Visited Alaska (board book)
* When Grandma and Grandpa visited Denali Natl. Park
* When Grandma visited Alaska
* When I Cruised Through Alaska
      * Old Maid - Alaska Style (card game)
      * Alaska Animal Block Puzzle (12-block puzzle)

Look at these books and games by visiting our website **www.alaskachildrensbooks.com**